Moon over the Mountain
Luna sobre la montaña

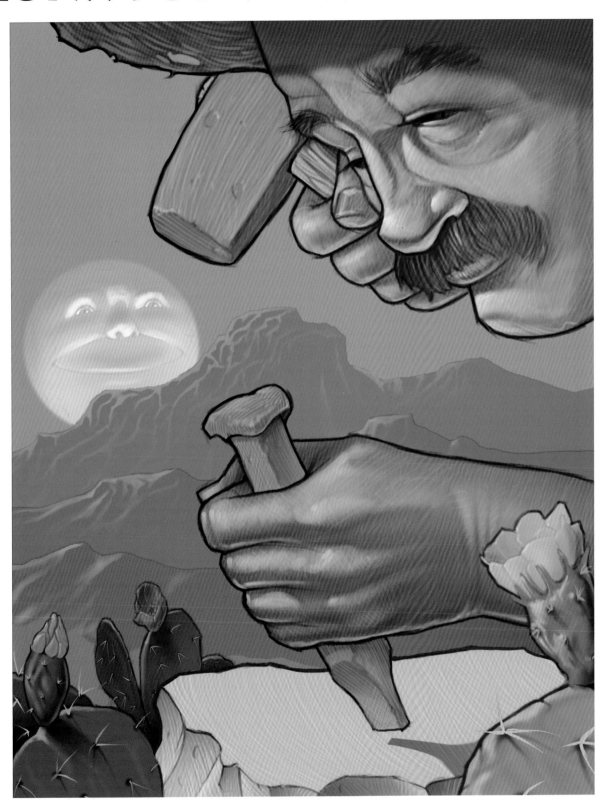

WRITTEN BY / ESCRITO POR KEITH POLETTE
ILLUSTRATED BY / ILUSTRADO POR MICHAEL KRESS-RUSSICK

For Anthony, Avery, Perrin, and Danikan. ✑ Keith

To Alan Russick, my father. ✑ Michael

Text © 2009 Keith Polette
Illustration © 2009 Michael Kress–Russick
Translation © 2009 Raven Tree Press

Polette, Keith.

    Moon Over the Mountain / written by Keith Polette; illustrated by Michael Kress–Russick;
    translated by Translations by Design = Luna sobre la montaña / escrito por Keith Polette;
    ilustrado por Michael Kress–Russick; traducción al español de Translations by Design.
    –1 ed. –McHenry, IL; Raven Tree Press, 2009.

    p. ; cm.

    SUMMARY: A retelling of a traditional Asian tale in which a discontented
              stonecutter is never satisfied with each wish that is granted him.
              Set in the desert Southwest.

Bilingual Edition
ISBN 978-1-932748-85-7 hardcover
ISBN 978-1-932748-84-0 paperback

English-Only Edition
ISBN 978-1-934960-07-3 hardcover

    Audience: pre–K to 3rd grade
    Title available as English-only and Bilingual text with mostly
    English story and embedded words in Spanish formats

    1. Fairy Tales & Folktales/Adaptation—Juvenile fiction. 2. Lifestyles/Country Life—
    Juvenile fiction. 3. Bilingual books—English and Spanish. 4. [Spanish language materials—
    books.] I. Illust. Kress-Russick, Michael. II. Title. III. Title: Luna sobre la montaña.

LCCN: 2009923416

Printed in Taiwan
10 9 8 7 6 5 4 3 2 1
First Edition

Free activities for this book are available at www.raventreepress.com

MOON OVER THE MOUNTAIN
LUNA SOBRE LA MONTAÑA

WRITTEN BY / ESCRITO POR KEITH POLETTE
ILLUSTRATED BY / ILUSTRADO POR MICHAEL KRESS-RUSSICK

Raven Tree Press
A Division of Delta Systems Co., Inc.
www.raventreepress.com

Agipito was a poor stonecutter. Day after day, he cut out stones for large houses and churches. Many casas grandes and iglesias were built with these piedras. Cutting stones was hard work, so Agipito longed for an easier life. But he thought his vida was set in stone.

4

Every day Agipito trudged up the great mountain
with his hammer and chisel. He chipped, shaped,
hacked, and hewed the piedras. Then he brought
the stones back to his small shop to sell. His
mercadito was at the base of la gran montaña.

6

One hot afternoon, Agipito was dragging a sled of piedras to his mercadito. As he wiped his face, he spotted the carriage of a rich merchant. Inside the coche, the comerciante rico was dressed in fine silk. Gold rings sparkled on his hands. El comerciante rico ate sweet fruit that Agipito had never seen or tasted.

"Oh, how I wish I was a comerciante rico!" Agipito said.

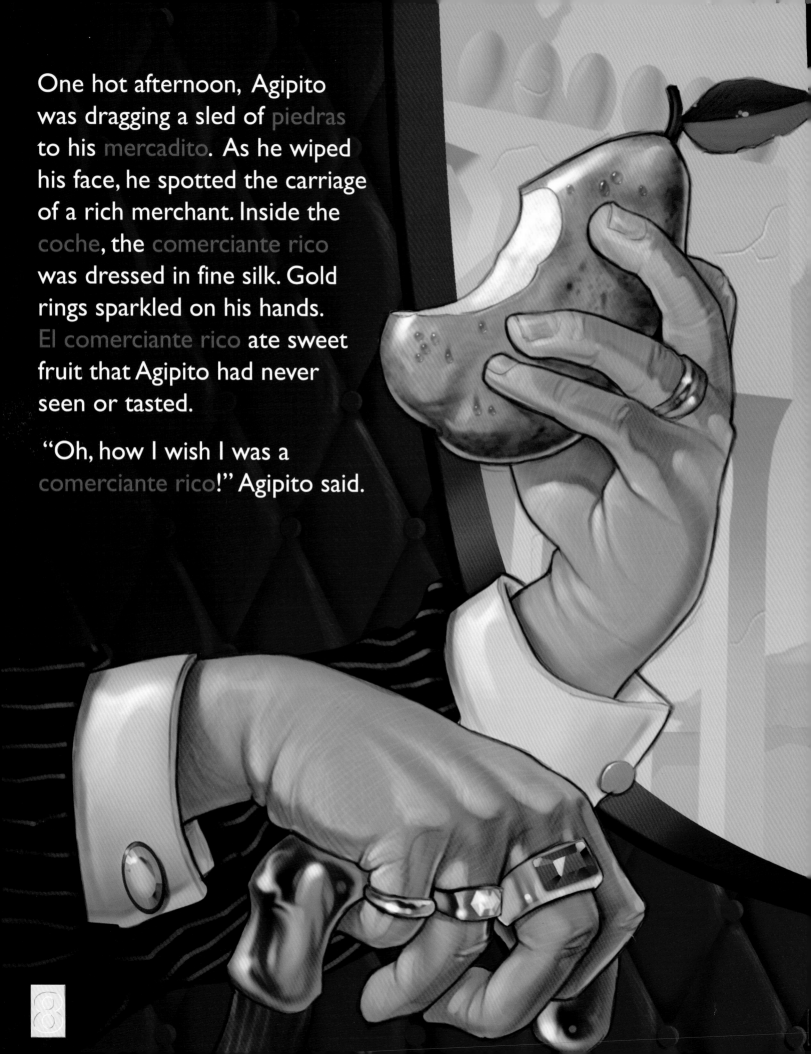

Agipito finally reached
his mercadito with the
heavy load of piedras.
Weary and worn, Agipito
went to bed early.

That night, the Spirit
of the Desert granted
Agipito's wish.

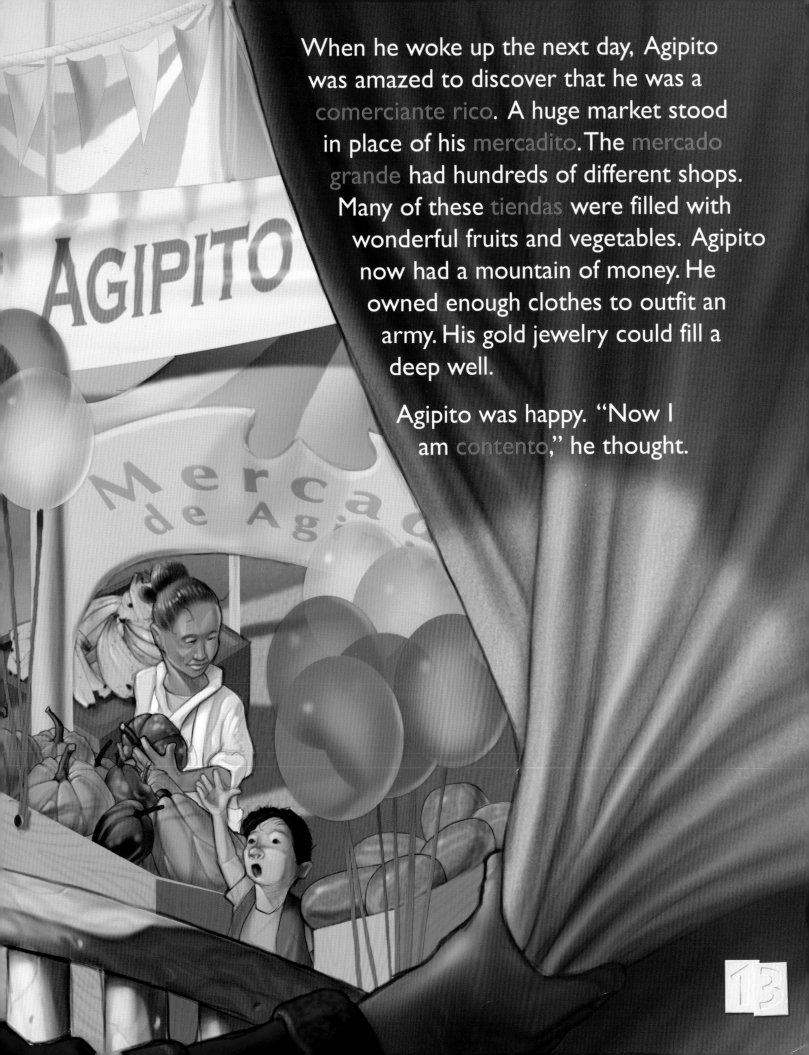

When he woke up the next day, Agipito was amazed to discover that he was a comerciante rico. A huge market stood in place of his mercadito. The mercado grande had hundreds of different shops. Many of these tiendas were filled with wonderful fruits and vegetables. Agipito now had a mountain of money. He owned enough clothes to outfit an army. His gold jewelry could fill a deep well.

Agipito was happy. "Now I am contento," he thought.

Agipito walked through his mercado grande as the sun blazed in the blue sky. Beneath the scorching heat of el sol, the sweet fruits and crisp vegetables in his tiendas wilted. The hand–painted fabrics faded. People fainted from the heat.

Agipito saw the strength of el sol and said, "How I wish I was el sol!"

As Agipito slept that night, the Spirit of the Desert once again granted his wish.

When he awoke the next morning, Agipito was el sol. He laughed with fire and hurled handfuls of heat across the land. The ground cracked and the crops withered. The rivers and streams ran dry.

Agipito was contento.

17

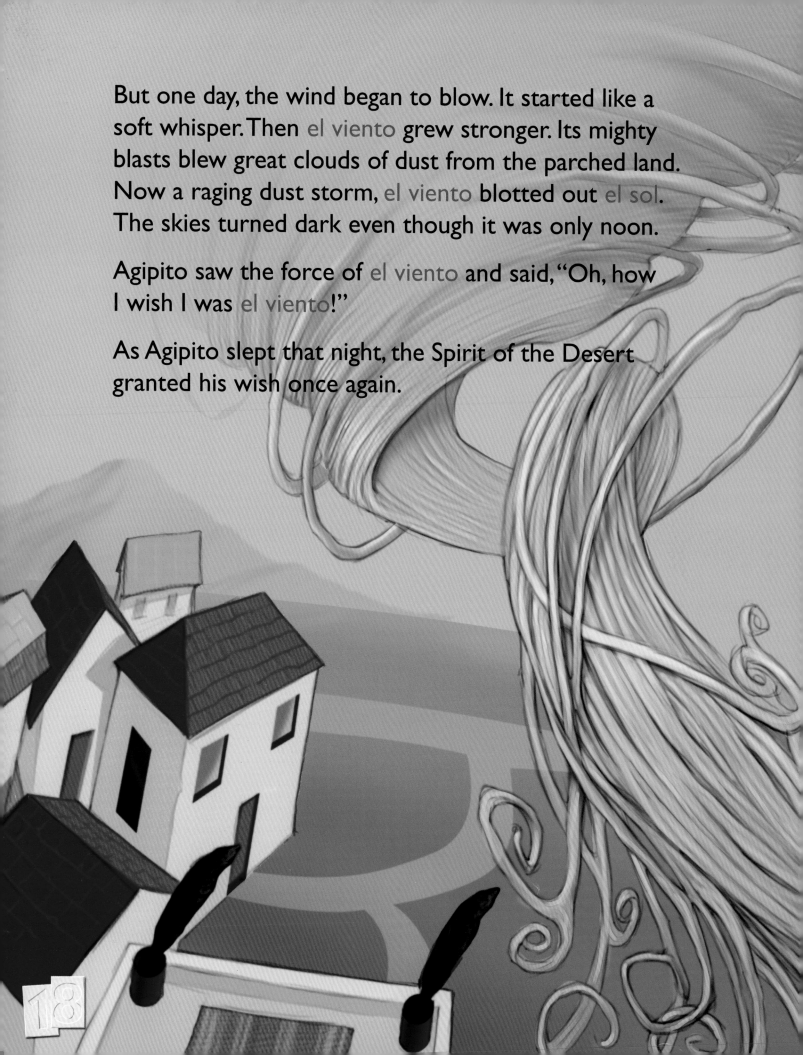

But one day, the wind began to blow. It started like a soft whisper. Then el viento grew stronger. Its mighty blasts blew great clouds of dust from the parched land. Now a raging dust storm, el viento blotted out el sol. The skies turned dark even though it was only noon.

Agipito saw the force of el viento and said, "Oh, how I wish I was el viento!"

As Agipito slept that night, the Spirit of the Desert granted his wish once again.

18

When the next day dawned, Agipito was el viento. He roared with delight and howled across the land. With his dust–filled gusts, Agipito sent coches and wagons tumbling. He blew down the casas that were not made of stone.

Agipito was contento—until he saw that la gran montaña stood firm.

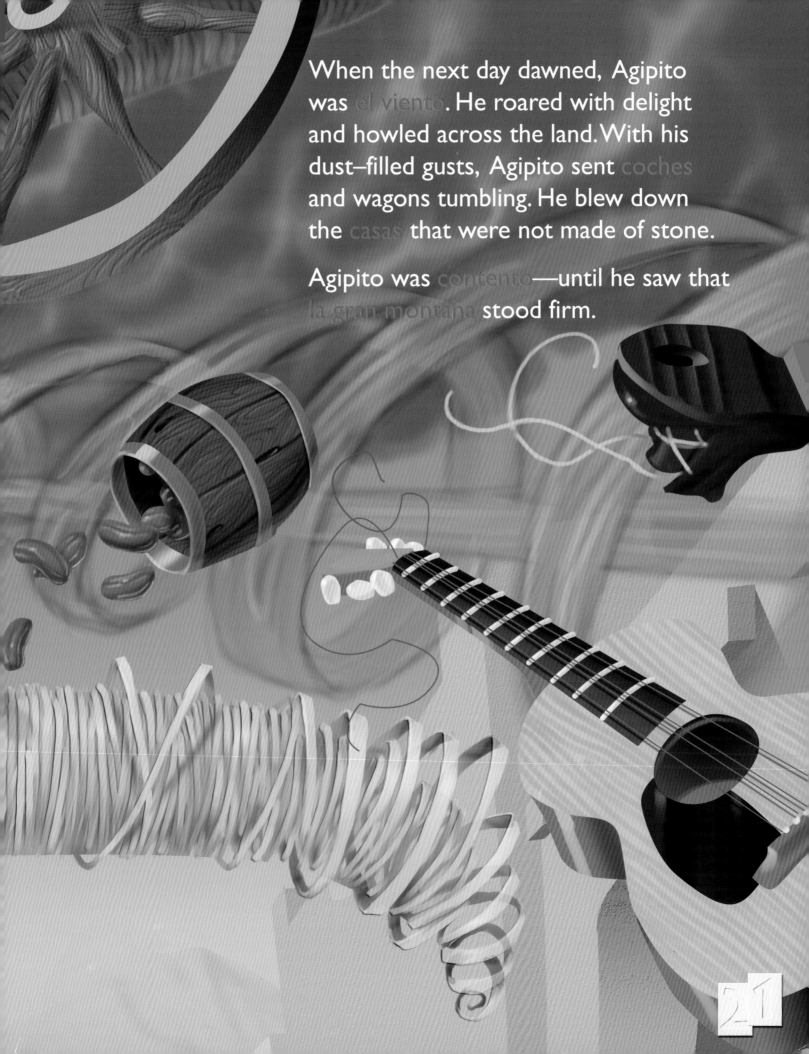

El viento unleashed a furious blast of wind against la gran montaña. But it did not budge. Agipito saw the power of the mountain and said, "How I wish I was la gran montaña!"

As Agipito slept that night, the Spirit of the Desert again granted his wish.

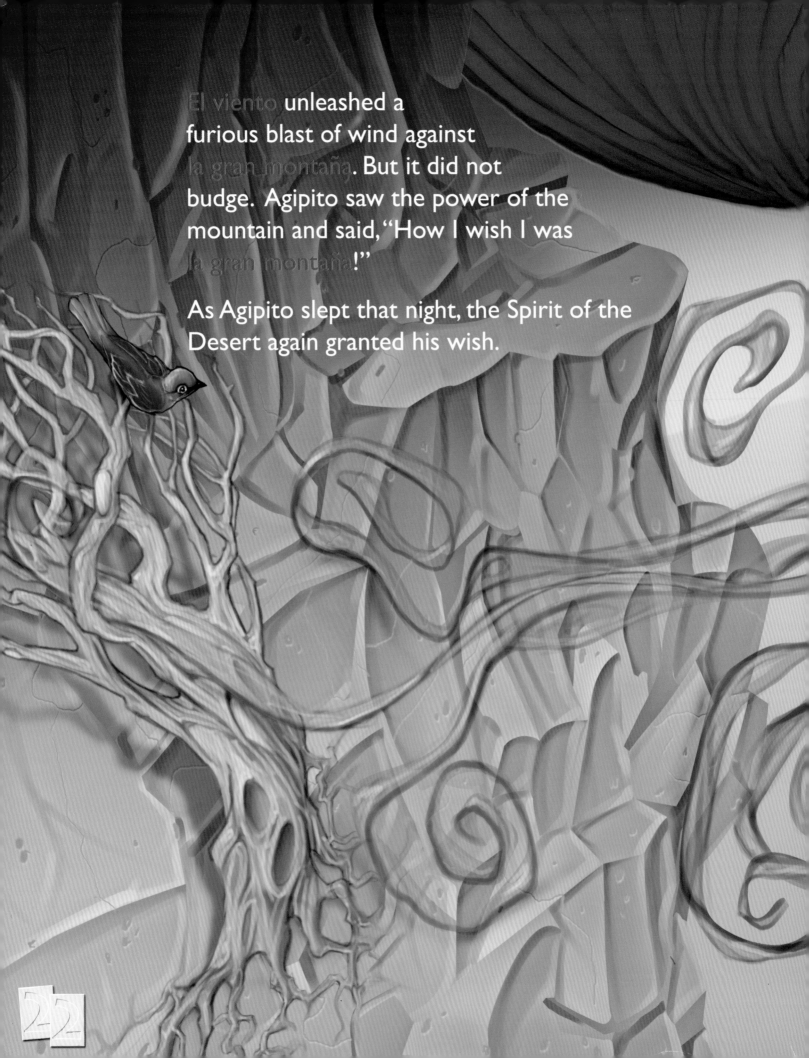

23

The next day, Agipito was la gran montaña. Agipito was now stronger than the comerciante rico, more powerful than el sol, and mightier than el viento. He proudly towered over the land.

Agipito was muy contento.

Early one morning, Agipito woke up to the sounds of a hammer and chisel. A poor stonecutter was hacking and hewing the piedras at the base of la gran montaña.

Agipito shuddered and made one final wish. The Spirit of the Desert granted it.

26

When Agipito opened his eyes the next day, he was a coyote. His fur coat was silkier than the fancy clothes of the comerciante rico. The eyes of el coyote flashed with the fire of el sol. His spirit was stronger than la gran montaña. His vida was no longer set in stone.

El coyote howled like el viento that night. As la luna rose over the mountain, el coyote disappeared into the sands of the desert.

He was muy contento.

31

Vocabulario / Vocabulary

casas	**houses**
grande	**great (large)**
iglesias	**churches**
las piedras	**stones**
vida	**life**
el mercadito	**small shop**
la montaña	**mountain**
coche	**carriage**
el comerciante	**merchant**
rico	**rich**
el mercado	**market**
tiendas	**shops**
contento	**happy (glad)**
el sol	**the sun**
el viento	**the wind**
muy	**very**
el coyote	**coyote**
la luna	**moon**